Princess
Coloring Book

Eileen Rudisill Miller

DOVER PUBLICATIONS
GARDEN CITY, NEW YORK

Meet the Princess

Imagine a young Princess who is kind, beautiful, and full of dreams and hopes. Then look on the next page and you will meet her! This delightful book will show you many scenes from her daily life. As you probably can guess, the Princess lives in a castle with her parents, the King and Queen, who are also pictured on these coloring pages.

What is it like to be a royal princess? As you enjoy coloring the pictures, you will discover that she wakes up in a bedroom that smells deliciously of flowers, and is decorated with candles and pillows. After saying "Good morning" to her parents, she has a tea party in the garden with her best friend. Later on, she has her royal portrait painted. She loves to read and play chess and cuddle with her pets, but she also spends time daydreaming. Do you ever wish on a star? The Princess does, too! And she can't wait for the dress ball. You will get to see—and color—the lovely gown that she plans to wear. Finally, you will learn that the Prince is a very special person in the Princess's life!

There are many more exciting scenes, so have your crayons and colored pencils or markers ready. The last few pages of the book contain a big surprise, so start reading now and you will soon find out what it is. Enjoy your visit to this fairy tale kingdom. Now, get ready to meet the Princess!

Princess Coloring Book first published by Dover Publications in 2012, is a revised edition of *Princess Leonora Coloring Book,* originally published by Dover in 2007.

ISBN-13: 978-0-486-49917-8
ISBN-10: 0-486-49917-0

Printed in the United States of America
49917015 2025
www.doverpublications.com

It’s a beautiful morning and the Princess
can’t wait to start her day!

As she brushes her hair, she thinks about the
upcoming dress ball. What will she wear?

The Princess loves to smell the flowers in the palace garden.

The Princess says "Good morning" to her parents, who are seated on their thrones.

The King and Queen are delighted to see their lovely daughter.

The Princess and her best friend chat as they have a tea party in the garden.

The Princess cuddles with her puppy, Maxwell, and her cat, Morgan.

Sometimes the Princess gets lost in a daydream. Do you?

Today the Princess had her portrait painted.
It looks just like her!

The Princess loves her gown for the dress ball!
She is looking forward to dancing with the Prince!

The royal carriage takes the Princess to the ball.

Doesn't the Princess look beautiful in her
sparkling necklace, earrings and tiara?

She arrives at the ball just as the stars begin
to twinkle in the sky.

Just as she had hoped—the Prince asks her to dance!

The couple glides across the floor as the King and Queen and the royal guests look on.

The night is full of enchantment for
the Prince and Princess.

Like many young people, the Princess
makes a wish and hopes it will come true!

May Day is one of the Princess's favorite holidays. It is a celebration of springtime.

The Princess and her friends take hold of a ribbon
and dance around the maypole.

The Princess finds some quiet time to read a book of poetry.

The Queen and King listen as their daughter
tells them about her wonderful day.

The Prince and Princess ride their horses
in the forest.

They enjoy the beauty of nature along the winding trail.

Knights on horseback take part in contests at the palace, displaying their bravery and skill.

The Princess awards a crown to the winner.
Who could it be?

Not far from the palace, the Princess and the Prince enjoy a picnic lunch.

After lunch, they play a game of chess.
Who will win?

The Princess's wish has come true—
the Prince asks her to marry him.

The couple shares the happy news
with the King and Queen.

The Princess waves good-bye and hopes that all of
your dreams come true, too!